This
Christmas Cracker
belongs to:

_____

_____

For Sophie
M.W.
For Felix
L.H.

First published 1997 by Walker Books Ltd
87 Vauxhall Walk, London SE11 5HJ
This edition published 2010
2 4 6 8 10 9 7 5 3 1
Text © 1997 Martin Waddell
Illustrations © 1997 Leo Hartas
The right of Martin Waddell and Leo Hartas to be identified as author and illustrator respectively
of this work has been asserted by them in accordance with the Copyright, Designs and Patents Act 1988
Printed in China
British Library Cataloguing in Publication Data:
a catalogue record for this book is available from the British Library
978-1-4063-3318-3
www.walker.co.uk

Mimi's Christmas

Written by
Martin Waddell

Illustrated by
Leo Hartas

WALKER BOOKS
AND SUBSIDIARIES
LONDON · BOSTON · SYDNEY · AUCKLAND

Mimi lived with her mouse sisters and
brothers beneath the big tree.

"Santa Mouse will come soon," Mimi told her
mouse sisters and brothers, as they huddled
up close to the fire. "You must write your
Santa Mouse notes, so he will know what
to put in your stockings."

The mouse brothers and sisters started scribbling their Santa Mouse notes.

They scribbled ...

and they scribbled ...

and they scribbled ...

and they scribbled ...

and they scribbled.

"I can't write Santa's note by myself, I'm too small!" Hugo told Mimi.

"I'll do it for you," said Mimi. "Tell me what to write."

This is the note Mimi wrote.

Dear Santa Mouse,
I hope you are well.
I'd like a BIG drum.
Love from
Hugo Mouse
X
P.S. I'm the small one.

"Does Santa Mouse have drums?" asked Hugo,
when they were hanging the lights on their
very own mouse Christmas tree.
"Well, he might have a small one," said Mimi.
"It has to fit in your stocking."
"A small drum that makes a big BOOM
when you bang it?" said Hugo.
"Just wait and see, Hugo," said Mimi.

Christmas Eve came and it snowed.
The mice tumbled and jumbled about
in the snow.

They tumbled …

and they jumbled …

and they tumbled …

and they jumbled …

till they all looked like little white mice!

"Supper!" called Mimi, and her mouse sisters and brothers came in from the snow. They had a Christmas Eve feast, huddled close to the fire with mouse lemonade and mouse cake.

"Let's leave Santa Mouse some," Mimi said, and she put mouse cake and mouse lemonade out for Santa, under the mouse Christmas tree in her garden.

"Time for bed, sleepyhead!" Mimi said.
Hugo hung up his mouse stocking at the
end of his little mouse bed. It was a very big
stocking, though he was a very small mouse.
"Is it big enough for my drum?"
Hugo asked.
"Just wait and see, Hugo,"
said Mimi.

The mouse sisters and brothers dreamed of
the toys Santa Mouse would bring for their
mouse stockings.

They dreamed ...

and they dreamed ...

and they dreamed …

and they dreamed …

and they dreamed.

All of them dreamed except Hugo.
Hugo was such a small mouse that he
felt too excited to sleep. He got out of
bed and he looked, but there wasn't a
drum in his stocking.

Hugo went looking for Mimi.
"I can't get to sleep and that means
Santa Mouse won't come," Hugo told
Mimi, and he started to cry. "There
won't be a drum in my stocking!"

Mimi took Hugo out to the garden.
"Santa Mouse always comes," Mimi said.
"He comes when our mouse world's asleep.
That's how Santa Mouse works."

Mimi put Hugo to bed. And the next morning...

BOOM! BOOM! BOOM!
"Hugo's got his drum," Mimi's mouse sisters and brothers told Mimi. And ...

Christmas was noisy at Mimi's!